MAGGIE SUZANNE
STAR OF CHRISTMAS

By Marilyn Goss

Marilyn Goss

ISBN No. 0-9620766-0-0

Printed in the United States of America
by Taylor Publishing Company, Dallas, Texas

DEDICATION

To Cindy, our precious daughter.

ACKNOWLEDGMENTS

With special thanks to my husband, "Tiny" Goss, whose love, prayers, and support always provide me with the strength I need.

To Ed and Gloria Shipman, founders and directors of Happy Hill Farm Children's Home in Granbury, Texas.

To Patty Wedding, Mike Slone and Barry Hayes for their special financial help and faith in my projects.

To Libby Patterson — the best help in the world — who runs our retail store, Marilyn's Art Room, in Waxahachie, Texas.

To Caleb Pirtle, III, an award-winning author, who helped me with some of the story concepts and who gave Maggie Suzanne her name.

And to the wonderful staff at Taylor Publishing Company, especially Helen Lance and Shawn McDonough.

Dear Friends,

I am so happy to share my first book with you! Many people ask if I am Maggie Suzanne. I don't think so, but I do know that a lot of Maggie Suzanne is me. Both of us are dreamers, thinkers, and doers.

I remember at a very early age how everything in life held a special interest for me. I not only saw rainbows in icicles, but even in the tiniest bubble. One of my fondest childhood memories is of bathing my face in the dew of each first May morning (an old May Day custom said to make one beautiful). And I remember then how the rainbows danced on the fresh morning dew.

My parents were wonderful Christian people who contributed to my love of the church and of all things spiritual. Christmas was always a favorite time of year in our home. Even though we never received many presents, we knew we were genuinely loved — and that was gift enough.

Maggie Suzanne's interest in the Christmas Story and her dreams of the Star are an expression of the way I still love Christmas. Maybe it's my response to Christmas that first brought the Light to my heart, as it did Maggie Suzanne. For it was Christmas that brought true love to the world.

My love for children led me into the field of education. I graduated from the University of Alabama with a double major in art and music. When I was young, I thought anyone could play the piano or paint. I never considered it a talent. It was just something I loved to do.

For fourteen years I was a public school teacher. But in 1968, I began to feel pulled toward a new direction.

On the way to school one spring morning, I pulled my car to the edge of the road and asked God for a sign to show me what to do with my life. Believing He gives direction, I should not have been surprised when into my art class flew a white dove. From the open window the bird flew toward the ceiling and made his landing on a heating pipe. From his perch, he calmly looked down upon my class of thirty-one astounded children, and on me, never offering to fly away or escape. We brought a long ladder, and one of the boys climbed up to try to capture the dove. As the boy reached up to get him, expecting a flurry of feathers and a rush of wings, the dove quietly stepped off onto his hand.

The experience moved me to reflect on my life and my prayer. Why did the dove come to my art class? What did it mean? I wanted to be able to pursue my art as a profession; yet I didn't have the courage to leave the security of my teaching position. However, I did resign, and believing this was my direction, began a new career as a professional artist.

The decision was a good one. For nineteen years I have followed this leading, and today my art is housed in fine collections around the world. And in each of my paintings somewhere is found a small white dove, along with an inspirational verse — a reminder of that spring morning when the sign I had prayed for flew into my classroom window.

In 1978 my work began to appear on Christmas cards. For ten years in a row, my paintings have been reproduced on benefit cards for Happy Hill Farm Children's Academy in Granbury, Texas, as well as the Wadley Institute of Molecular Medicine in Dallas. In the first four of these paintings the same children appear. It is from this series that Maggie Suzanne was born. These paintings are the basis for this book, and are reproduced in the story as they were inspired.

As you read this very special story, may all the joys of Christmas shine in your hearts — as they do in Maggie Suzanne's.

Merry Christmas,

Marilyn Goss

Marilyn Goss

MAGGIE SUZANNE at last fell asleep. The Christmas storybook lay by her bedside. All night long she had dreamed about the Star that had led the Wise Men to Baby Jesus. She dreamed it was still there, and she dreamed that she had found it.

When Maggie Suzanne awoke from beneath her warm, goose-down comforter, the clock told her she had slept far too long. She jumped out of bed and ran to the window.

"Surely the Star must be there," she cried. "I want it to shine on me so I will be special, too." But Maggie Suzanne was sadly disappointed. There was no Star; only billions of snowflakes. "I wonder," she thought aloud, "where do the stars go when it snows?" But the only one to answer her was Tabigail, her pet cat, who was still fast asleep. "And anyway," thought Maggie Suzanne, "what does a cat know about stars?"

Maggie Suzanne dressed quickly in the chilly morning air. She did not want to be late for school again. Grabbing her hat, she hurried to the closet to get her warm coat, boots and scarf. All of a sudden, she thought about Jingles in the barn. Jingles was her very special pet goat. "He will be cold today," Maggie Suzanne worried. "And he might freeze if I don't take care of him."

So she and Tabigail took grandmother's favorite quilt out to the barn to cover Jingles. Jingles was so funny. He just crawled out the other end of the quilt, thinking to himself, "What's the matter with Maggie Suzanne? Doesn't she know that God gives animals special coats in the wintertime so they don't need grandmother's favorite quilt?" Even so, Maggie Suzanne lovingly tended to all her animals.

Hurrying through the snow towards the little red school house, Maggie Suzanne could

hear the school bell already ringing. "Oh dear!" she exclaimed. "I hope I don't miss

the Christmas Story today." All the children loved to hear the teacher tell the Christmas

Story. She told it each year the day before the Christmas holidays began.

Maggie Suzanne was singing and catching snowflakes with her tongue when the red brick

wall appeared. "Maybe," she thought, "if I could climb to the top of this wall,

I could see the stars." But when she jumped up on the wall,

all she could see were more snowflakes.

And there was something else she didn't see . . .

. . . the other end of the wall! She tumbled off into the soft snow. Almost without missing a step, she jumped up and ran as fast as she could to catch up with the last arrivals to school. Maggie Suzanne was always running late. But somehow, it seemed, she was always just in time.

When she opened the door of the classroom, Maggie Suzanne heard the teacher calling her name. Breathlessly, Maggie Suzanne answered, "Present!"

Now with the boys and girls in their proper places, the teacher began, "For unto us a child is born . . ."

How thrilled the children were to hear about that special Christmas Day.

Everyone felt like singing. "Are you going caroling with us after school, Maggie Suzanne?" they asked at recess time.

"Of course," Maggie Suzanne replied excitedly.

"I wouldn't want to miss that for anything."

"Don't be late!" they shouted.

For unto us a child is born

8

After school Maggie Suzanne rushed to the barn with a Christmas ribbon in her hand. She wanted Jingles to look his best for the caroling. She had heard the other animals would be there, and Jingles must go so he could hear his favorite song, *Glory to God in the Highest.* Maggie Suzanne sang it to him all the time — a bit off key, and a little too loud — but Jingles loved it. In fact, Jingles loved almost anything Maggie Suzanne did.

As she finished tying the Christmas bow, Maggie Suzanne heard a noise from inside the barn.

Rudy the rooster was crowing for all he was worth! "Rudy, what's the matter with you?" called Maggie Suzanne. "This is not the time of day to crow." As Maggie Suzanne and Jingles drew closer, they could see something moving in the hay. Florabelle, the nanny goat, had just given birth to a newborn baby.

Suddenly, the little goat wobbled to its feet. "What a beautiful baby you have, Florabelle," Maggie Suzanne whispered as she reached to pat the mother gently on the head. She stood there a moment, thinking about the Christmas Story. "I wonder how it must have been on the night the Christ Child was born? What did the manger look like? Was it like this barn? How did the baby stay warm?" Florabelle's baby had a special coat like Jingles to keep it warm.

The Christmas Story said Baby Jesus was wrapped in swaddling clothes. Maggie Suzanne thought that must have been a very special coat. On that night the angels had sung, *Glory to God in the Highest;* on this night, Rudy was crowing just as if he, too, knew the song.

"You certainly don't sound like an angel singing," Maggie Suzanne teased him. But Rudy thought he did, and Florabelle did, too. "Jingles, we've got to hurry now, or we'll be late for caroling," said Maggie Suzanne.

When they came to the edge of the barn, Maggie Suzanne looked up to behold the most beautiful icicle she had *ever* seen. Suddenly, a rainbow formed in the icicle, and Maggie Suzanne stood mesmerized in the snow. As the setting sun moved rapidly across the horizon, the rainbow changed, shifting its brilliant colors.

"Well, you cannot run away and leave a rainbow, can you?" thought Maggie Suzanne. The caroling could wait, but the miracle would not.

"Look at this rainbow, Jingles," Maggie Suzanne whispered, with marvel and wonder in her voice. Jingles looked up, his eyes sparkling in the fading light. He loved the rainbow, too.

FAVORITE CAROLS

The stars were beginning to appear in the night sky as Maggie Suzanne and Jingles hurried down the lane toward the carolers. Maggie Suzanne looked up and thought for certain she saw the Star, but she was too late to stop. There was no time now for the Star to shine upon her. All the children were in their places, their high, sweet voices singing *Glory to God in the Highest* as Maggie Suzanne and Jingles arrived at the house.

When they had finished singing, one of the children said, "Maggie Suzanne, you're late again." "Yeah," said another, "you're always late. We sang the whole song without you." "I know," apologized Maggie Suzanne. "We really tried to get here, and we did make it just in time to hear you sing Jingles' favorite song, *and,* we were just in time to see the miracles!"

"What miracles?" asked one of the boys. But it was time to sing again. Maggie Suzanne suddenly remembered she had left her caroling book in the barn. It didn't matter anyway. She knew most of the words, and with the memory of the miracles in her heart, she had many songs to sing.

Glory to God in the highest

'79 © Marilyn Goss

16

The next day was Christmas Eve when everyone in the village presented gifts to the Christ Child. Maggie Suzanne looked at the clock. She had played in the snow most of the day, and now it was almost time to go. Through the frosted window she saw some of the others trudging through the deep snow, carrying their gifts to the church.

"Oh, dear!" cried Maggie Suzanne. "I forgot to get a present." She looked around her room filled with beautiful dolls and toys. From her closet she took a box that was just big enough for any of her nice toys. Yet, somehow she didn't think any of her things were quite appropriate. Then she remembered the Christmas Story. "I know what I will do," she said, running for the barn.

"Here Gertie, here Gertie!" called Maggie Suzanne. Gertie was her Christmas goose. "Hold

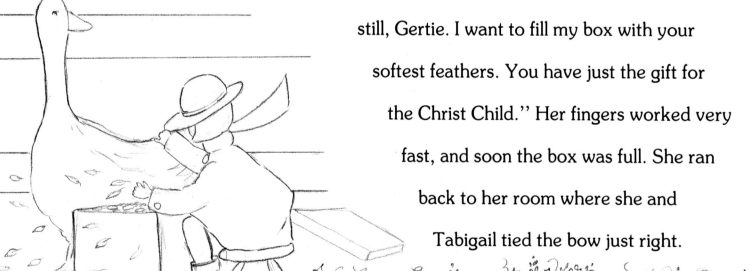

still, Gertie. I want to fill my box with your softest feathers. You have just the gift for the Christ Child." Her fingers worked very fast, and soon the box was full. She ran back to her room where she and Tabigail tied the bow just right.

"Now," Maggie Suzanne suddenly realized, "I must think of some way to get to church in a very big hurry." She knew she could never trudge through the snow as the others were doing and hope to make it in time for the service. "I know," she said. "Florabelle would love to have some exercise. The baby wouldn't miss his mother if I borrowed her for a little while."

Quickly, Maggie Suzanne went back to the barn. The sled that had been used for fun on many snowy days would be perfect to carry her gift to the Christ Child. She knew it was always in the barn loft, safely put away. There was no time to lose.

Florabelle knew something special was happening when Maggie Suzanne reached for the harness. After Maggie Suzanne tied the Christmas bell around Florabelle's neck, they were ready to go.

Maggie Suzanne squealed with glee as they raced over the ice and snow. "I know we will get there on time now," she declared. "What a beautiful night!" The clouds had rolled away and the sky was filled with brilliant stars. "We're making such good time," Maggie Suzanne decided, "we may even get there early."

Suddenly she saw something in the sky. "Whoa, right here, Florabelle. Look at this! There it is! That must be the Star of Christmas." The Star sparkled like a giant diamond in the sky. Maggie Suzanne lay back on her sled. She wanted to feel the beauty of this magical night.

Florabelle was happy to stop, for she had found a small bush to nibble on. This was Maggie Suzanne's chance to let the Star shine upon her. But then she thought, "It doesn't seem right to ask His star to shine on me. That was just for Him."

She was still and very quiet for a few moments as she studied the entire sky. "Florabelle, have you ever wondered what all the other stars are for? There must be a jillion. Surely they have some purpose."

She thought and thought.

Florabelle munched and munched.

"I know!" Maggie Suzanne, exclaimed suddenly. "I know why they're up there! Every time a new baby is born in the world, God places another star in the sky." Florabelle understood. "I wonder which one is for your new baby, Florabelle?" Most of all Maggie Suzanne wondered which one was for her and which ones were for her friends. She could hardly wait to get to church to tell the Good News.

Maggie Suzanne was late again, but so were some of the others as they plodded through the deep snow. Maggie Suzanne walked into the church just in time to open her gift. As she carefully lifted the lid from the box, some of the feathers began swirling about the room. Everyone began to laugh.

"What a dumb present," sneered one of the boys. "Hey, look! Maggie Suzanne brought a box full of feathers," laughed another. "We brought nice things, like dolls and toys."

Maggie Suzanne explained, "You don't seem to understand. These are not just feathers. This is goose down. I read in the Christmas Story that the Christ Child had no place to lay his head. I haven't had time, but I'm going to make him a pillow. Goose down makes the softest pillows on earth."

The children stopped laughing and took another look into the box. "What else do you have in there?" asked one of the boys. On top of the feathers was a piece of the icicle, still frozen and shimmering in the glow of the church lamps.

"I brought Him the rainbow, too," revealed Maggie Suzanne. "And on the way to church tonight, I found the Christmas Star. I also discovered that God has placed a special star in the sky for each one of us."

In the past, the children had always made fun of Maggie Suzanne for what she said and did . . .

...they presented unto Him gifts...

1980 © Marilyn Goss

But on this Christmas Eve, the children walked all the way home — each one looking

o the sky for his own special star. And each one felt surrounded by a very special kind of love.

Maggie Suzanne looked and looked, but she could not find anything special to put on the tree. Disappointed, she sat down in front of a mirror and looked at herself. "Maybe I'm wrong. I can't find *anything* special. Maybe no one has a special star. Maybe I will never, ever, be special, either."

Then Maggie Suzanne noticed her grandmother's picture on the wall and realized how much she looked like her. She remembered the light she had always seen in her grandmother's face. And then she remembered the Christmas Story. It said, "He is come a Light into the world." Her grandmother had that Light. Maggie Suzanne looked again into the mirror and saw the same Light in her own face.

Suddenly, she sat up straight and tall, startled by her own discovery: it is not the Star that shines upon you that makes you special — but the Light that shines within you.

C hristmas Day dawned bright and beautiful. Every year Maggie Suzanne and her friends would choose a tree in their neighborhood to decorate. This year they chose the giant evergreen in front of Maggie Suzanne's house. They came inside to get a better view of the tree and discuss exactly how to begin the decorations. Each child decided to bring a special ornament for the tree. They searched in the attics of the neighborhood houses to find just the right one.

Filled with the joy of her discovery Maggie Suzanne grabbed her hat and headed outside toward the tall ladder leaning against the huge tree. Excitedly, she began to climb higher and higher. She knew in her heart she had found the only special ornament she would ever need . . . *herself.* The sunlight coming up over the little church danced on the bright, white snow. It was the beginning of a new Christmas Day. It was the dawning of a new Light.

Maggie Suzanne climbed as far as she could go; then she stepped off the tip top of the ladder and onto the highest boughs of the giant evergreen. She was holding on for dear life, determined to get to the very top. She didn't let the wind or the swaying of the tree stop her. Only by looking up could she keep her balance.

Little by little she inched her way to the top. Just as she reached the highest branch of the tree, the church bells began to ring in the valley. Maggie Suzanne was just in time to become the Star of Christmas.

I am come a light into the world

1981© Marilyn Goss

31